Arnold Green, Dionysios Solomos

Greek and What next?

An address. Solomos' Hymn to Liberty, a Poem

Arnold Green, Dionysios Solomos

Greek and What next?
An address. Solomos' Hymn to Liberty, a Poem

ISBN/EAN: 9783744722056

Printed in Europe, USA, Canada, Australia, Japan

Cover: Foto ©Andreas Hilbeck / pixelio.de

More available books at **www.hansebooks.com**

GREEK AND WHAT NEXT?

AN ADDRESS.

COLOMOS' H

A

READ

ALUMNI ASSOCIATIO

JU

A

SIDN

" A decline in the state of Greek scholarship implies even more than the failure of esteem for the most valuable and influential of all languages; it involves with it a gradual but certain decay of general culture, the sacrifice of learning to science, the neglect of the history of man and of thought for the sake of facts relating to the external world."—*Isaac Todhunter, Conflict of Studies, p. 135.*

Gentlemen of the Alumni Association. In asking one to speak before you, whose daily life is removed from academical influence and collegiate association, and in assigning to him a subject peculiarly fitted for academical discussion and collegiate decision, you certainly do not expect from him either learned disquisition or technical argument. The claim of the classical languages to a place in our schools, has been so often disputed and so vigorously defended, has for so many generations been the theme of writers and speakers, has gathered around itself so huge a literature, that the studious critic finds nothing left to say. Year by year we read statements and counter statements, that were as familiar to Michael Neander and Jerome Wolf, as they are to the teacher and learner of to day. Nay more, in this long dispute between the defenders of what is called the old, and the partizans of what is styled the new, in this continued conflict of studies, from Erasmus of Deventer to Herbert Spencer of London, I do not believe that anybody has ever convinced anybody else. For the difference between the disputants is not in detail, but in substance; is radical, not merely superficial. On the one side, we are told, that the object of boyhood's training is to open vistas of varied learning and so to strengthen the neophyte's sight, as to enable him to scan the broad horizon of mental achievement before he chooses his own special pathway of labor, to harden his intellectual fibre, and to form judgment and taste, without reference to definite ends, to prolong and broaden preparation in the belief that future work will reflect and return the long labor of discipline, and the long years of hopeful teaching and study. On the other, we are reproached with wasting the plastic period of youth in pursuits which bring no reward, in employments which compared with the demands of active life, are trivial and trifling, in studies which rather unfit than prepare the student for the world in which he must soon struggle to obtain success, or it may be to maintain his existence. The plea for years of study to ensure knowledge, which must be gained before life's work is begun, or be given up forever, is answered by a demand for early fruit, and for such speedy and special training as may insure its production.

The education, which is general, involves a long period of labor and waiting that contributes little to the student's support, and is therefore beyond the reach of large classes in every community. It thus becomes to them an object of envy or distrust or, perhaps, dislike. Having no sympathy with it, they possibly gain a repugnance to it, and the theorist's dream is used as a foil to bring into bolder relief the useful work of the practical laborer. Again, the prospect of speedy reward is the strongest incentive to work in minds that cannot as yet have been accustomed to the interval between seed time and harvest, and long waiting in patient labor breeds discouragement, which induces belief that a new age demands a new training; that a modern society calls for modern methods; that the old is worn out, and that all things should be made new.

Of the classical languages, the more elaborate and the more perfect one has been selected, of late years, for special attack. The Latin is grudgingly allowed a place among useful studies, at least as yet, but the advocates of a reformed education demand the exclusion of the Greek from our schools and colleges so far as it is a part of the regular and required courses, and the substitution for it of some modern language or of some scientific study. Greek has been selected as the weak point to attack, and I believe it to be the most important in our whole educational system. I come before you, gentlemen, accepting your invitation to address you in the spirit which prompted you to give it, and I come to express my gratitude that our collegiate course circled around the classical languages, and to confess my own conviction that had boyhood received more Greek, manhood's work would be better done.

Yet I congratulate those who love the classics that there are men as able, as acute, as enthusiastic in other departments to watch their performance and to criticize both their methods and their results. The alertness of an antagonist is the best earnest of faithful work, his aggressive opposition the best assurance of honest labor. I hope that the classical instructor and the scientific teacher will each maintain his respective cause with unabated interest and unfailing zeal, that the dispute between them will neither cease nor grow less warm, that neither will allow the other to rest in routine or to drown vigor in the bitumen lake of a mediæval dialectic. Certainly the humanist may look back over the last century with unalloyed pleasure. Decade after decade, our schools have demanded more from their pupils, and the response has been ready and easy. More Latin and more Greek, more science pure and applied, more modern languages have been put into the required courses, and the student has increased his acquisitions without exhaustion. The masters of knowledge have themselves set the example, and the success of classical scholars has quite equalled that of their scientific rivals. As Lavoisier and Davy reformed chemistry, Friedrich Wolf reconstructed Greek learning and Gustav Hugo rewrote Roman law; Humboldt designed and executed his encyclopædic manual of science, and by an intellectual grasp of detail not less amazing, Niebuhr recognized and Gœschen and Bethmann–Hollweg deciphered the palimpsest of Gaius. While Kirchhoff at Heidelberg was blinding himself with the study of the solar spectrum, Ritschl at Bonn was rediscovering the text of Plautus. Rowan–Hamilton gave to mathematics a new instrument of research, and Laurent completed his wonderful commentaries on the civil jurisprudence. Our own generation has, with bewildered surprise, followed the observations of Charles Darwin, and read the inscriptions of August Bœckh and Theodor Mommsen. Nor has less energy been shown in the humbler tasks of classical learning. Frere and Rogers have compelled Aristophanes to talk English. Jowett has again translated Platon and has tried to translate Thoukudides. Prendergast and Dunbar have finished their concordances of Aristophanes and of Homeros. Wide as may be the differences, earnest as may be the dispute between the scientist and the Grecian, the outcome of their discussions must be good so long as each feels the inspiration of his own study and the stimulus of his opponents' criticism to acquisition and production.

But we must not imagine that the dispute can be concluded, and the disputants reconciled. The scientific school and the classical cannot coalesce. They differ in the choice of studies. They also differ in the modes and in the aims of study. The one is special, the other general. The one assumes a chosen field of work, and prepares the student to till it. The other knows nothing about the student's ultimate intentions, and cares nothing for them. The one dismisses its pupil with a certificate of preparation for his future work. The other admonishes him that his broader study must be supplemented by his technical training. To substitute the scientific school for the classical is merely to build the superstructure at the expense of its foundation to let an easier and a shorter discipline take the place of a severer and a more prolonged. If the additional time gained for a practical branch of education secures greater depth of acquirement, this advantage is offset by the loss of that breadth which is even more important to youth. Of course, in dealing with the higher education we must assume the student's ability to give to it the necessary time, just as the existence of the higher schools implies wealth and leisure and culture in the community which supports them. The classical school could not exist in a purely industrial society, dependent for its daily support on its daily labor.

The choice then urged upon us is between a preparatory education that is general, and one that is special; between a course of study which is built up on the Greek as the most perfect language for the expression of human thought ever used by man, the language underlying all modern literature and permeating all western culture, and a course that substitutes for the Greek something, the acquisition of which involves less labor and requires less time. I say build up on the Greek, for its influence upon the Latin was so strong that to one ignorant of it, Roman literature is meaningless, and Roman history, during the periods in which Roman action and Roman thought have most affected our own, becomes unintelligible. I say build up on the Greek, for broad culture involves Greek learning by an implication more close and necessary than I fear even some of our instructors are willing to admit. Without Greek the very name of classical education becomes a misnomer. One half of modern and mediæval life can be explained only by reference to Roman letters, Roman thought, and Roman law, and all these drew their inspiration and much of their matter from that long roll which contains the records of Greek genius, beginning with the marvellous songs of the Homeric Skalds, and for us ending with the splendid harangues of Chrusostomos.

With the choice thus presented, as with all questions regarding the higher education, popular demand has nothing to do. The decision must come from the comparatively small body of educated men, whose training has enabled them to form and defend their opinions from familiar knowledge. I am inclined to think that our professed collegiate practice fairly corresponds to their views. I do not over-

2

look the prejudice, if you please so to call it, the natural
feeling which may lead them to regard the training which
they have received, as the best for others, nor do I disregard
the feeling which prompts those who have not enjoyed their
advantages to consult their experience and follow their
advice in order that a child may secure more finished culture
than his father could obtain.

Thus far, I am glad to say, those who demand the excision
of one or both of the classical languages from our school
programmes, have failed to obtain the support which they
professed to expect. Forty two years ago Francis Wayland
wrote,[1] " The colleges, so far as I know, which have obeyed
the suggestions of the public, have failed to find themselves
sustained by the public. The means which it was supposed
would increase the number of students, in fact diminished it,
and thus things gradually, after every variety of trial, have
generally tended to their original constitution. So much
easier is it to discover faults than to amend them, to point
out evils than to remove them; and thus have we been
taught that the public does not always know what it wants,
and that it is not always wise to take it at its word." This
criticism on the changes made in one Massachusetts college
and afterwards to be tried in another, was prophetic of the
fate of his own plan introduced here eight years later.
Some of you remember the care with which it was arranged,
the brilliant anticipations which attended its adoption, and the
completeness of its practical failure. Not less suggestive is
the history of the school which Julius Hecker founded in
Berlin in 1747.[2] He endeavored to combine in a single
institution, preparatory courses for the universities, courses
of instruction for students, who, not intending to pursue
university studies, wished to be fitted for military life, or
civil, artistic, mechanical or agricultural, and also courses
for others, who, as artizans or peasants, desired a merely
elementary education. Three departments partly coördi-
nate and partly graded, a German, a Latin and a Technical

furnished the machinery. The effect at first was to develop inordinately the technical division, which provided teachers in arithmetic, geometry, mechanics, architecture, drawing and natural science, and soon furnished special teaching in nearly every branch of work. An effort seemed making to teach everybody everything. After twenty years of trial the death of its founder put the school into other hands. The new Superintendent rearranged the departments, and gave to them their characteristic names of German or Artizan's School, Art School and Paedagogium. The two former continued their work with ample provision and a minuteness of detail which approached caricature. Meanwhile, term by term, the paedagogium, following the irresistible law of its development, assumed more and more the peculiarities of a general classical school, until just fifty years after its creation it deserved and received the name of the "Friedrich Wilhelm Gymnasium." In 1811 it was formally separated from the other departments of the former foundation.

In urging the radical difference between our classical schools and those demanded by our so called reformers, in insisting upon their incompatibility, and in thus illustrating it, I should anticipate your criticism by an explanation. The special preparation of a German student is understood to begin with the university. He selects his department of study at his matriculation, and is supposed during his university career to be preparing himself for his own life's work. Everything before the university, work in the progymnasium and gymnasium, whatever names they bear, is general education leading up to the special university training. With us this special preparation begins after graduation from college. All before this, study in the preparatory school and the college under whatever names, is general culture. So that our graduate, when he receives his academical degree, corresponds pretty nearly in development and in age with the "abiturient" of the foreign gymnasium. Bearing this in mind, we may, I think, properly cite the experience of others as well as our own.

What is to be the future of our American colleges, is an interesting and not wholly profitless subject for speculation. Some of them, with the aid of age and wealth, will probably surround themselves with special schools for final training, until these become grouped into a proper university which the college will feed with its graduates, and for which it will become a preparatory academy. Others, I think, while increasing the number of departments and of their teachers, will stop short of the university development and grow into large schools, either technical or classical; possibly, if their endowments permit, uniting the two more or less closely under a single government; probably, confining their educational efforts to one of these two different objects; preparation for a university and preparation for active life. Meanwhile the colleges are bearing the double burden of general and also of limited training, perhaps carrying on neither so well as they might were the other removed. While this state of things lasts we cannot quote the old practice and urge the presumptions of experience in its favor, for the past and the present may be quite transitional; and many institutions are like, many men, the fact that they exist is no good reason why they should continue to be. We may, however, refer to our experience as showing that the higher culture is more in honor among us than the lower, that the general education is more in demand than the special, and we may be contented that the influence which blessed us, is still exerted to elevate culture, not to depress it; to broaden education, not to narrow it; to extend discipline, not to contract it.

With most of the familiar objections to Greek study I have no patience whatever. I do not know whether to be amused or vexed at seeing a brilliant scholar like Robert Lowe select from the rich armory of Hellenic culture the very weapon with which he assaults it; but when we are seriously asked, in the alleged interests of scholarship, to substitute German for Greek, I cannot help doubting whether the request comes from one able to read either of the two languages. Shall Greek be abandoned on account of its inutility, a reason which the accomplished Legaré truthfully and keenly called the fundamental and ultimate argument of the opponents of classical education,[3] then what is to take its place? Exact science? But are not the practical affairs of this world managed by men who are as ignorant of determinants and quarternions as they are of Greek, who recognize as little distinction between differentiation and integration, as they do between the Ionic dialect and the Attic? Is therefore the calculus to be given up, then what becomes of physics and mechanics? Is Greek to be rejected, then what becomes of the humanities? Or natural history? to be pursued in ignorance of its vocabulary and its terminology? Will the scalpel of the anatomist and the lens of the botanist give a knowledge of the development, the structure and the classification of animal and plant which will compensate the student for his inability to follow the intellectual development of man, the structure of society and the classification of thought? Or systematic politics? Can their history and spirit be apprehended by one who knows nothing of Aristoteles, who has never studied the independent statelets of Hellas, or looked for the source of that administrative wisdom which made the Byzantine government keep the standard and weight of its gold coinage unimpaired from Constantine to the crusades,[4] who has never made the Strasburg of Maurer and the Ghent of Froissart a commentary upon the Kerkura of Thoukudides? Or modern literature? Can its achievements be understood by a reader unable to comprehend the debt which Milton owes to Euripides, Gray to Pindaros, Tennyson to Theokritos, and I beg you not to misunderstand me, Swinburne to the choral lyrics of Aristophanes?

But we are told that our Greek study is not only useless but wasteful; that it is so conducted as to leave the student, after the instruction of years, unfamiliar with Grecian thought, and unable to read with ease an ordinary Greek page. If the latter is true, the former certainly is, for language is the key to the spirit's casket. The, statement is serious, and it should have serious consideration, for I fear that it contains a most uncomfortable and a most unnecessary amount of truth. Many of us, who after receiving our degrees, were sent to continue our studies at continental schools, can recall the feeling of surprise and discouragement with which we took up the work imposed on us by the daily lectures that we attended. Instead of the few pages we were wont to spell out with the aid of lexicon and notes, our professors threw at us Latin and Greek by the chapter and the book, and they expected us, day after day, to follow them and to read their references. Our companions in the lecture room, no older than ourselves but trained in their native schools, were able to do it; we were not, until we had spent in laborious drudgery, months which should have been otherwise employed. For my own part, I shall never, during life, forget the feeling of heart sickening indignation with which I saw others who had studied no longer and no harder perform tasks beyond my own power, and with which I turned back to work which ought to have been long before finished. Great changes and great improvements have doubtless been made in our modes of teaching and study during the last quarter of a century, and I do not wish to be unjust; but I appeal to those of you who twenty five years ago went from an American college to a German university, to corroborate or refute my statements. How many of you endured the torture of a similar experience? Now this was all wrong, and the more wrong because remediable. I do not believe that learning to read Greek is more difficult than learning to read German, so far as the vocabulary is concerned, and the subtleties of expression in any language are only appreciable to one who has read much and carefully. I do not know whence came the idea that the classical languages, unlike all others, are themselves ends and not means; are the adytum and not the vestibule of learning.[5] Nor do I know why a student, if properly taught, should not, after four or five years of study, be able to read ordinary Greek with ease. Does he? For this question is pregnant with the fate of our classical studies, and with the destiny of our liberal schools. If our boys are trained to use Greek as a tool and to use it readily, I do not believe that it can ever be supplanted by anything. If they are not, it is quite possible that the advocate of classical education may hereafter find difficulties in his way harder to contend with than any which he has heretofore met; difficulties which our instructors will either prevent or create.

Of the two classical languages, Greek is certainly the more difficult; and yet, in the circular of one of our large preparatory schools, I read but a few days ago that Latin was studied for six years and Greek for three. The necessary result of this is clear. Would it not be better to allot five years to Greek and four to Latin? Karl von Raumer tells us[6] that in the school at Stendal the different teachers gave weekly forty five hours of instruction in Latin and twenty three in Greek; in the school at Erfurt, forty two in Latin and twenty one in Greek; in the school at Koesfeld, sixty one in Latin and twenty eight in Greek; and that these figures embody the practice in the other gymnasia. Perhaps these figures explain the dissatisfaction with the work of even these German schools, expressed or implied by several of the faculties of those nine universities which gave to the Prussian Minister of Education, toward the close of the year 1869, their formal opinions on the admission of graduates from the technical schools to university degrees. That the standard of classical education is higher in Germany than with us, only makes the subordination of Greek to other studies in our schools more surprising. What can we expect, if the easier language is to receive twice the time allowed to the harder, assuming that instruction in the easier one is economically given and is not excessive? Again, how many of our boys are taught that Greek is studied to be read, not to serve as an admission ticket to college? How many of them are compelled to use those modes of becoming familiar with words and sentences, rhythm and sense, to which we all resort in studying a modern language? How many of them are required to read Greek aloud, or asked to memorize the brilliant verses of the scholia or the anthology? Again, are they not forced to rely too much on the dreary rules of syntax, and to lose the grammatical knowledge only obtainable by a wider acquaintance with the classical texts? "The aorist was made for man, not man for the aorist," and I incline to think that the portions of a foreign grammar which become parts of ourselves, are those learned from reading which is not a task, rather than from syntactical systems, whose very aspect is repulsive. The great Melancthon followed the instinct of a profound scholarship in ending his school grammar with the paradigms of the verbs in μι. I wish that our college teachers could introduce the seminar. The labor would be discouraging for a time, but, if persistent, would reap a rich reward. It was in the seminar that Wolf, at Halle, educated Boeckh and Bekker. The recent presentation of the Oidipos at a neighboring university, was a pleasant proof of continued interest in Greek letters and a cheering illustration of profitable work, not so much in the exhibition of old costume and the old stage, though this was curious, as in the close acquaintance with a great drama, the familiarity with its construction, its details and its expression, which the participants could perhaps have gained in no other way. The representation became thus academic work of the truest and most fruitful kind. Again, do not our professors, at times, deal with Greek in their classes as an element in comparative philology rather than as an introduction to Hellenic letters and Hellenic thought? No honor is too great for philological science. Its masters have opened a new volume in the history of man, and have read to us pages of the fresh-

est and most vivid interest from the old records of society
and of thought. They have illumined their work with pict-
ures of the brotherhood of races of the kinship of languages
and laws. They are the keepers of the archives of humanity,[7] and yet the student ought to read easily the text of at
least some of those archives before he is led to philosophize
on their contents. Their achievements are in a special department of labor, and Greek is the corner stone of a general education. I can imagine a classical teacher with math-
ematical tastes leading his students in their Greek studies
to the writings of Eukleides or Apollonios or Diophantos.
His work could not be called wasted, for these men pushed
their science up to the limits which were to confine it for a
thousand years; but would this be a legitimate use of Greek
school study? Would it not be an attempt to specialize
what ought to be kept general? Again, are not our preparatory schools sending their pupils to our colleges at such
a stage of classical acquirement as to hamper the professor
and trammel the student alike, so that the instruction which
the one wishes to impart and the other should desire to receive, can be neither given nor assimilated? An experi-
enced university teacher once told me that his whole effort
was directed to the middle third of his class. The first third
did its own work, the last third was hopeless, while the in-
tervening third received all the instruction. And it is this
middle third, the typical average of the school and of life,
which liberal education does most to strengthen and to
broaden, which profits most from the teacher's skill. Have
our preparatory teachers, in their instruction and guidance,
remembered that, under the old "trivium," grammar meant
criticism and history as well as word form? Have they
borne in mind the often repeated question of Edward Free-
man, Why do our boys know so much of Miltiades and Leon-
idas and Pausanias and so little of Aratos and Kleomenes
and Philopoimen? Or have they thought that a like query
might apply to Latin study also? Five men lived under the

3

Roman emperors, the influence of whose intellectual work on the after history of Europe has been greater than that of all the rest of the Latin writers put together. Every school boy is familiar with the names of Cicero and Horatius and Tacitus, but he hears little of the debt which he owes to Gaius and Paulus and Ulpianus, to Modestinus and the great Papinianus.

The specialization of study, when allowed to begin, proceeds with an accelerating and dangerous rapidity, often helped on by the inclination of both teacher and pupil, the one pursuing his hobby and the other his tastes. It is the business of a liberal culture to prevent it, and each department of this culture must be carefully guarded against it. If it controls a school, general education can no longer find there a proper training ground. If it takes possession of a department of study, instruction becomes partial and one sided. The teacher learns at the student's expense, for the teacher has passed out of his general studies into his own special ones, and makes the discipline in these more severe and more engrossing. Just the rigid and absorbing study of mathematics, which has made English Cambridge famous, prompted Hamilton, of Edinburgh, to call that school a "slaughter house of intellect."[8]

If a boy's home life is subject to educating and elevating influences, his school work may be made of the most general kind. He may be trusted to learn, untaught, much that is given by elementary education, and he will certainly learn it. If his circumstances enable him to pursue liberal studies for the usual time, he may safely, during the years of preparation for college, confine his school labor to Greek, Latin and mathematics, and if physical weakness or accidental interruption requires one of these to be given up, I would regretfully but unhesitatingly cut out the Latin, for, necessary as it is in the study of science, of history, of literature and of the Romance tongues, still it is less important than the Greek, and its acquisition in later years requires less pro-

longed and less irksome toil. But the condition of success
in this classical discipline is that the boy should learn to read
the ancient languages, both of them as a rule, the Greek,
if but one can be studied, and to read them until confidence
in his power to understand has taken the place of distrust.
Of course this involves two things not always found coinci-
dent, that the pupil should be an earnest student and that his
teacher should be a mature one. Of course too, this involves
the mastery of manifold difficulties ; arising from the subject .
matter which is studied, and I have no wish to represent it as
easy ; from the student's idiosyncracies, which are often very
trying to the teacher; from the student's environment, the
influence of which is potent for good or evil ; and from the
teacher's peculiarities ; the old idols are all here of the tribe
and the cave of the forum and the theatre, but where in life
can we escape them ? The labor is arduous, but the reward
is great.

And moral rewards, which are obtained by faithful and
successful struggle, far surpass the expectations of the aspi-
rant. They are governed by a rule the direct opposite of
that which agricultural economists call the law of diminish-
ing returns. Recorded experience seems to show that classical students who have profited by proper teaching, are
better fitted for the pursuits of technical science, far better
for those of the so called learned professions, than students
specially trained from the beginning of their studies for their
special departments. I have already alluded to the reports
made in the year 1869, by nine German universities, to the
Minister of Education in Prussia.[9] The universities were
Kœnigsberg, Berlin, Greifswald, Breslau, Halle, Kiel, Gœttingen, Marburg and Bonn. Each of them has a theological
faculty, a legal, a medical and a philosophical, but at Bonn
and Breslau there are two theological faculties, one Protest-
ant and one Roman Catholic. The question submitted to
them was, whether, and how far graduates of the technical
schools should be admitted to the universities as candidates

for university degrees. This meant whether students without Greek, and with less Latin than is taught in the classical schools, should be received in the universities on the
same footing as students from the gymnasia. The theological faculties unanimously answered no. Seven of the legal
faculties answered no, those of Kœnigsberg and Gœttingen
answering yes. Five of the medical faculties answered no,
and four, yes. Four of the philosophical faculties answered
no, two of them yes, and the other three were in favor of receiving the technical students upon certain expressed condi-
tions. December 7, 1870, a ministerial order directed that
the testimonial of a Prussian technical school of the first rank
should be received in the Prussian universities like the testimonial of a gymnasium, so far as Prussians were concerned,
intending to devote themselves to the study of mathematics,
natural science or modern languages, under the philosophical faculties. March 8, 1880, the philosophical faculty of
Berlin, after an experience of nearly ten years, unanimously
requested the minister of education to reconsider this order.[10] The memorial of request distinctly asserts that the
gymnasial graduates had shown themselves better fitted than
the technical for the departments of study open to them both,
that the classical students outstripped the technical in the
higher mathematics, astronomy, chemistry, descriptive natural science, the English language, the German language,
philosophy, political economy and statistics. This action is
made very significant by the fact that between 1869 and 1880
the faculty had greatly changed and had much increased its
membership. The opinions of 1869 expressed by one body
of men were ratified in 1880 by the experience of a practically different body. Prophecy was fulfilled in history. We
may learn a like lesson from recent experiments in France.
A government circular of September, 1872, and a law of
February, 1880, reduced the school time allowed to the
classics and prescribed courses of instruction in which the
French language held a secure preponderance. Four years

have elapsed since this change was consummated, and the first of French reviews[11] is already sounding an alarm. The standards of examinations have fallen, not only in the provincial schools but even in the Sorbonne, and a French scholar asks for the revision of the school programmes, not in the interest of the classics, but for the sake of general French culture and of the French language itself. Add to this that Zupitza, of Berlin, states, in his faculty's request of March, 1880, that he often found a difficulty in teaching the English grammar to those of his students who were unfamiliar with the Greek, which he did not meet with in the case of the classical graduates, and the advocates of classical study may, I think, rest satisfied. Those of us who believe in Greek felt that we were right in claiming for it acknowledgement as an integral part of liberal education, but we could not have looked for such testimonies as these. Greek has been selected as the point of attack, but selected because it is the salient bastion of the whole educational line.

The student's indebtedness to Greek begins with the first hour of his reading when he first tries to understand words rich in derivatives of every kind, inflected with every shade of meaning, and combined with prepositions and particles which are his despair. He believes that the sentences express definite ideas, but he cannot easily be persuaded that given words have any fixed significance, or that their collocation is determined by anything save the writer's will. When he has overcome this skepticism and has learned that prepositions in their manifold combinations and uses, and the whole bewildering multitude of particles, all denote or connote ideas; that the nouns and verbs do mean something, and do present by their changeful forms the lights and shades of thought, he has practically mastered all the grammar which the Western scholar needs. The freedom of the Greek sentence, in contrast with the rigid construction of the Latin, makes the one seem a formula, of which the other illustrates a subordinate rule. There language is subjected

to thought, and follows its direction in a path straight or
crooked. Here language and thought move over the or-
dered rails of rule. The study of Latin is exercise in lin-
guistic geometry : that of Greek is discipline in the calculus of grammar. This flexibility of grammatical construction gives to the student his first great difficulty. After
he has so far mastered it that it ceases to be a constant em-
barrassment, he begins to understand the absolute power
with which the Greeks made their language the slave of
their thought. In reading even the greatest of the Latin
lyrics, I think we are conscious of the writer's skill and feel
a pleased surprise at his success. I think our impulse is to
wonder that confined in the unyielding framework of syntactical law the poet can so lovingly make the sparrow peck
the finger tips of Lesbia, so gracefully promise a young
Torquatus to his parents' prayers, so wildly wail the lament
of Attis through the Phrygian groves ; but when the Greek
song writer wraps the myrtle around his sword blade, as did
Harmodios and Aristogeiton, or when the choir of the Hip-
polutos chants the destined misery of Phaidra wrecked on
her awful woe, we are conscious of neither poet nor metre.
The closing scene of the Prometheus bound, is sublime in
its grand defiance, but the poet's language is lost in the
poet's thought. Attempt to translate it ; your English mind
fails to grasp the relation of the demi god to the Supreme,
you have broken the connection between feeling and utterance, and your words will be either · bombast or rant.
Brilliant as are the writings of Tacitus, full of meaning and
irresistible in their attractiveness of condensed wisdom and
cold epigram, the style is still obtrusive, the author is stand-
ing between his subject and his reader. Turn to Thoukudides and the author has disappeared, the student is com-
muning directly with the writer's ideas. There is no style,
only page after page of sentences, whose grammatical structure is bursting with the pressure of the thought which has
been crowded into them, till the reader doubts whether the

master workman wrestled with a language as yet unformed, or was lost in his work and wrought on reckless of grammar. Among the Latin prose writers, Cæsar, in his commentaries, shows perhaps the most perfect subjection of language to thought, but Cæsar was the most perfect Greek of them all.

That a language of surprising flexibility and wealth, of great power and grace, typical in its characteristics of the people who used it, mirrors the development of a race which was unrivalled in its skill of adaptation, its perception of symmetry and its love of liberty; that this language reflects the spirit of an ancient culture which has become part of our own, shows to us those masterpieces of intellectual workmanship which are recognized models of literary invention, construction and presentation, is the medium through which the master minds of a remote past have made us the heirs of their thought; that this language differs from our vernacular as much as two allied languages can differ from each other, and yet is one of the elements which are combined in our modern English; is a sufficient vindication of its study. Yet all this does not express the claim which the Greek has upon us. Our chief debt is not to the Greek tongue, but to the Greek genius, to its science and art and letters; its geometry and politics, its temples and statues, its history and literature. It dealt with every department of intellectual work, and in each its mission was to broaden, to adorn, to invigorate. It gave to its ministers a birth gift of breadth, beauty and strength, in virtue of which they still do and ever will live.

Look, for example, at the speech in which Lukourgos attacks Leokrates, for violating the orders adopted in behalf of the public safety, after the disasters of Chaironeia. "Three things," says the speaker, "make up the State, the ruler, the judge, the citizen, and each of these has bound himself to the others by oath, for men may be deceived, but the gods cannot be. Wherefore the Greeks at Plataiai,

when drawn up against the force of Xerxes, bound themselves by an oath not then devised, but imitated from the
one which is habitual among you, which it is worth while
for you to listen to. Let the clerk read it." *" Ού ποιήσομαι
περὶ πλείονος τὸ ζῆν τῆς ἐλευθερίας.*[12] . . . ." I will not value
life more than liberty. And we can hear echoes ringing
through the annals of our own land from the words of the
old Puritan of Athens.

The great philosopher of the Academy taught his pupils
to look beyond life and across its surrounding boundary of
death. As he closed his Politeia with the rewards and punish-
ments which Er saw distributed in vision, so he closed his
teaching by boldly lifting up the veil of the infinite. You
recall the noble words with which his followers uttered their
loftiest thought in the opening sentence of that manual so
familiar to you, which Platon himself would have rejoiced
at could he have lived to see it : *"'Εν ἀρχῇ ἦν ὁ λόγος καὶ ὁ
λόγος ἦν πρὸς τὸν Θεόν καὶ Θεὸς ἦν ὁ λόγος."* In the beginning
was reason, and reason dwelt with God and God was reason.
Shall we recognize the evangelist as the follower of the philosopher, or shall we look on the Platonic dialogues as an instruction to the Sermon on the Mount?

The orations of Isaios are one of the wonders of literature. They are professional arguments on doubtful and
technical questions of the Athenian law of inheritance, on
subjects bristling with legal difficulty and repellant with legal formality. Yet they have taken their place in the polite
letters of the world. True, similar successes have been won
since. Witness a few of the arguments of the half dozen
greatest advocates who have used our own language ; witness, too, the Mercuriales of the Chancellor D'Aguesseau,
and you may judge from these how great is the triumph of
the Attic lawyer. Nor is he alone in his power to give last-
ing interest to a discussion of themes whose importance
seems transient. Isokrates and Demosthenes have described
the business dealings of the banking house of Pasion, and

their narratives read like an article from last month's review. Nor is this world spirit which arrests decay and keeps the passing ever fresh, found only in the work of the master craftsmen. The verses of Theognis can make no pretension to greatness in any way. I doubt if they even belong to literature proper, and yet they are so full of that unexpected commonplace which makes up life, the expression is so plain and so like the thought, and both so like ourselves, that we read, half wondering if we have not seen it all before, perhaps in last week's magazine.

Greek poetry and Greek philosophy are trite subjects. Let us for a moment confine our attention to the orators, for what is true of them applies also to those who have in other branches of work, made the Greek name immortal.

The breadth and strength of Greek oratory are more striking to us than its beauty, but are, in fact, not more characteristic of it. The broadness and vigor of its workmanship vibrate sympathetic chords in our own minds; hence we appreciate these excellencies without trouble, hence, too, we can analyze them without difficulty. Let me cite the words of two writers, both accomplished scholars, both celebrated authors, both familiar with Hellenic work, and yet the mental antipodes of each other. Edward Bulwer, in his oration before the undergraduates at Edinburgh,[13] said of Demosthenes, "Many speakers have literally translated passages from his orations and produced electrical effects upon sober English Senators by thoughts first uttered to passionate Athenian crowds. Why is this? Not from the style, the style vanishes in translation. It is because thoughts, the noblest appeal to emotions, the most masculine and popular." Edwards Park, in his address on the life of Leonard Woods, tells us,[14] "Clear thought deeply felt, and having possession of the speaker who has possession of himself, is eloquence." Put these statements together and they explain much of the power of the Attic speakers. The extent of their mental grasp whence came their utterance, the

4

virile vigor of their feeling which controlled their hearers. the limpid clearness of their ideas and language, account for much, but much still remains, all of their beauty.

We Teutons have an idea, which the uneducated mind thoroughly believes in, and with which even the educated is somewhat tinctured, that strong appeal on grave subjects is or should be the result of what we are pleased to call inspiration, that good speaking is extemporaneous, and that the orator loses dignity and power by dependence upon previous preparation. Jebb, in his introduction to the Attic orators, attributes this to the Hebrew element of our education,[15] emphasized by the reformers, and I suppose due to the Old Testament in our vernaculars. I am not sure that he is right, for the idea is older than the reformation, and too deeply rooted not to have great antiquity. If Hebrew in its origin it may have come by direct tradition through the mouths of the great rabbis of the Ashkenazim and the Sephardim, but it more probably is a survival from the times when our forefathers recognized the prophetess and obeyed the Aurinias and the Veledas[16] of old German story.

The Greek conception of the speaker's task was quite different. According to it the speech is a work of art, and the speaker an artist. In mastering the subject matter, in arranging the mode and order of presentation, in determining the style and expression of delivery, no drudgery of labor is excessive, no detail of preparation is trivial. This study of matter, of arrangement, of delivery is perhaps what the great Athenian meant when he defined oratory by a three-times repeated "ὑπόκρισις."

The beauty of the Greek orators springs from their having so fully realized this conception, which I believe to be the true one. Before we can appreciate it we must put off something of the Germanic and put on something of the Hellenic. We must truly feel that symmetry and simplicity are essential elements of the speaker's success, as well as earnestness of thought and speech. If we can do this, the Greek orators will find in us at least enough of the spirit with which they were once heard, to secure admiration for their massive strength and love for their honest and perfect beauty, beauty of expression in words which are the hand-maidens of thought, beauty of thought which traverses its subject like sunlight in a path direct and clear.

And those who listened to these Greek speakers were trained into full sympathy with them by an education probably the broadest and the most thorough to which a free people ever submitted. We have heard a great deal about the influences surrounding an Athenian boy, how he lived amid the masterpieces of architectural and plastic art; how the masters of thought kept open schools to instruct him by their conversation; how the masters of speech were constantly addressing the people, of whom he was one; how the masters of poetry were ever illustrating the history and faith of his race in the great theatres, where he sat all day listening to elévated sentiment and polished verse. Rhetoricians have described these things as if they believed the Greek citizen to be a lounger, who received his culture by simple absorption. But for forty years of his life, from twenty to sixty, the Athenian was at the command of his government, in peace and war, for deliberative discussion, for judicial decision, for religious festival and for military service. At eighteen[17] the boy passed from his father's care into the hands of the State, and for two years received a compulsory preparation for every department of the citizen's duty. He was kept under arms in the field and in garrison; he was obliged to attend the courts and the assemblies; he was forced to study under the grammarians, the orators and the philosophers; he was made a participant in the State religion, twice he sang in the procession of the great Goddess of Eleusis; a sharer in the State festivals, twice in honor of the great dead he marched to the mound at Marathon and to the shore opposite Salamis, and when he was admitted to citizenship there was nothing in his public du-

ties which had not been made familiar to him. All this
breadth and strength of educational purpose, and for ends
political and practical, characterized the routine life of a
people that we too often regard as only artistic and visionary,
as boasting of a freedom which it degraded to license. There
are certainly passages in the annals of free Greece which I
would not willingly defend, but if we strike out those which
fall under the four hundreds, and the thirties, and the
τύ ραν, they are very few in number. I do not believe
that history can show a State which more perfectly realized
than did Athens, the proud words which its historian puts
into the mouth of its statesman: "φιλοκαλοῦμεν γάρ μετ'
ἐυτελείας καὶ φιλοσοφοῦμεν ἄνευ μαλακίας,"[18] which more ideal-
ized man's actual life, which so kept vigor and so combined
with it grace. It was the Attic Greek who first conceived
the perfect man of our own later and Christian civilization,
and called him the "καλός κ' ἀγαθός," the elegant and the
good.

Moreover, the symmetry of the Greek intellect forbade a
partial training. As if to anticipate the lament of a subse-
quent age, that modern life requires so much of those who
live it, the Greeks found that society demanded from its
members all the vigor of a well disciplined mind, all the
endurance of a well trained body. They gave to the physical and the metaphysical equal care, and tended them both
in the same spirit. There is neither materialism nor sensu-
ality in the songs which Pindaros sang of the victorious
athletes. It was neither of these things, I think, which
gave rise to the story of Hupereides unveiling Phrune before
the judges of the Areiopagos. The Greek sense for the
beautiful in form is beyond our apprehension. We can not
imagine the pleasure with which the Greek eye followed
the perfect development of perfect figures, or the delight
with which it watched the sinuous movement of steel like
muscles that undulated in their play beneath the surface of
a healthy skin. I frankly wish that we could. We should

then make parts of our education strong which are now weak. The Greek training affected the very aspect of the race, for while the Greek woman was white, the Greek man was brown, and meanwhile the vigor of mind and the vigor of body acted and reacted on each other. Later the Stoic, and still later the Ascetic, in their contempt for the physical left behind them a baleful influence which we still feel, but if these bodies of ours are the instruments with which our mental and moral work is to be done on earth, if they are creations in the image of the Creator, if they are temples of the Holy Spirit in us,[19] there is no greater nonsense than to regard them with indifference or to speak of them disparagingly. Mentally, morally, physically, I would gladly see our boys moulded in the type of that marble hero who stands at the end of one of the Vatican galleries, leaning on the head of the conquered boar, his figure instinct with the spirit of Hellenic thought and of Hellenic art, muscular, masculine, comely, complete.

But can the study of Greek be changed with inutility, even by the most practical of reformers who demands the most practical of results? Generation after generation boys have left our schools trained by Greek and its companion Latin, some of whom have displayed in their after lives the breadth, the strength and the beauty of mind, will and character which made them living illustrations of how the past teaches the present, of how the present vivifies and reproduces the virtue of the past; have borne into life's contests the humanity of classical learning, have decorated life's triumphs with the elegance of classical grace. It may be that daily duty left them little time for communion with the ancient teachers of boyhood. It may be that these teachers grew strange to the sight of later life; but the work of teaching was still done. The loaf is none the less leavened because the yeast plant is killed in the oven's heat. Nor do I shrink from examples. If of the men in our land who have recently passed from the stage of action, I was asked to say whose lives typified the Greek spirit which I have referred to, whose honors were the fruitage of severe classical discipline in youth, I should give the names of Horace Binney and Charles Francis Adams.

In all great mind work there is something which overlies all mere mind training, something which we feel but cannot grasp, which we can neither define nor analyze. We are conscious that it is present, but we cannot tell why. We yield to its power, which we can neither explain nor criticize. It is strong, subtle, impalpable. Let me illustrate, for this something completes our indebtedness to the Greek. You remember how a score of years ago two men well known in public life, met at a solemn festival in the outskirts of a little town in Pennsylvania, one learned, accomplished and scholarly, full of the doctrines of the schools, the finished rhetor in New England's history; the other of all this the opposite, void of learning, accomplishment and scholarship, yet I ask you to weigh the ten minute speech of Abraham Lincoln in that graveyard at Gettysburg, against the two hour oration of Edward Everett, and to tell me if there is not in pure literature something which no education can give, if there is not even here something of more value than all culture? Of the classical languages, it is the crowning glory of the Greek that this something Demosthenes and Platon had, Cicero and Seneca lacked. If my illustration surprises you, open your Thoukudides and you will find that the fire which glows through the words of Lincoln was kindled by Perikles to honor the Athenian dead.

Fellow graduates of the University, again and again we have met to find the hope of years once before us changed into the experience of years which we have left behind, to miss well known figures, and to see vigorous forms pressing on to take the places of those of us who are falling, or have fallen. As we occupied the seats that our fathers once filled, our sons are now sitting where we sat in yonder halls.

We look at the familiar scenes and greet each other with our hearts full of that feeling which made the aged Kreousa weep over the cradle of her boy. The problems of preparing for life and of performing life's duty, which long ago we thought in boyhood's way were weighty and urgent, now press upon our minds with a tenfold force, for it is not of ourselves that we think, but of those, flesh of our flesh and blood of our blood, who are soon to take from our hands the torch of our culture to speed with it through a new generation, and to hand it in turn to others yet unborn. This yearning that our children may be wiser and stronger than we is more than a wish that they may enjoy the excellencies which we imagine that we have, and be free from the defects which we know that we labor under; it claims, and you will recall another old Greek thought, the performance of a duty not to ourselves, not to our children only, but a duty which the citizen owes to his State. It is for us, so far as we can, to take care that our successors may go forth into life panoplied with the wisdom of the past, to battle as paladins for the good, the beautiful and the true. Have we done our all to make ourselves fathers of such children as we would fain have? Are we doing our all to make our children such as we wish them to be, for we must remember that we and they live under the reign of a law as inevitable as fate, as inexorable as justice, as eternal as God. What our fathers were, we are; what we are, our children must be. The best, the most fruitful, the most effective methods of school training are matters to us not for ornamental debate, but of intense and imminent interest. Where can we find the influences, whither shall we look for the models, whence can we draw the spirit, of a culture whose discipline may give to healthy and hopeful minds a strength which will not fail in the strenuous struggle, a breadth which will not attenuate in the grooves of routine, a beauty which will not fade in the arid years of drudgery, a culture which may become an inspiration to youth, a comfort to wearied manhood, a support to reflective age?

Brothers Alumni, have I done rightly in pleading with you for the Greek? May I ask you to look up the long arcades of time and see those fair creations, the Εὐφροσύνη and the Σωφροσύνη as they walk toward us from a distant past, accompanying an older and a grander figure, cheering and relieving the august austerity of the Hebraic Torah, and may I remind you that the joyousness of conscious preparation, the self restraint of conscious ability, and the conviction of conscious duty, are the three things which carry man through all the work that man does well. Shall we not then, mindful neither of the difficulty of the labor nor of its length, nerve ourselves to fulfill this duty to our children and the State before the night cometh, when no man can work, before we, too, must abandon our tasks, and join our fathers who have gone before us where

" ἕνα πάντες ἀεὶ θᾶκον συνέχουσι καὶ ἕδραν
ἀντὶ βροτῆς ἄβροτον, κάλλιμον ἀντὶ κακῆς."[20]

1. Noah Porter. The American Colleges and the American public, pp. 14-16.

2. Karl von Raumer. Geschichte der Pædagogik, vol. 2, pp. 167-171.

3. Hugh S. Legaré's Writings, vol. 2, pp. 22, 26,

4. George Finlay. Greece under the Romans, pp. 533, 534. Byzantine Empire, vol. 2, p. 389.

5. Hieronymus Wolf. "Sunt enim latina et graeca lingua non tam ipsa eruditio, quam eruditionis fores aut vestibulum." Karl von Raumer, Geschichte der Pædagogik, vol. 1, p. 430.

6. Karl von Raumer. Geschichte der Pædagogik, vol. 3, p. 61.

7. Martin Wohlrab in the Neue Jahrbuecher, vol. 110, p. 368. "Die Hauptlehrer am Gymnasium sind die Philologen. Was sind Philologen? Kurz gesagt, die Archivare der Menscheit."

8. Isaac Todhunter. Conflict of Studies, p. 238.

9. Akademische Gutachten ueber die Zulassung von Realschul-Abiturienten zu Facultæts-Studien. Amtlicher Abdruck. Berlin, 1870, Verlag von Wilhelm Hertz. 8vo. pages 112.

10. Die Frage der Theilung der philosophischen Facultæt. Rede zum Antritte des Rectorats in der Aula der Friedrich-Wilhelms-Universitæt zu Berlin am 15 October, 1880, gehalten von Dr. August Wilhelm Hofmann. Zweite Auflage mit einem Anhange: Zwei Gutachten ueber die Zulassung von Realschul-Abiturienten zu Facultæts-Studien, Sr. Excellenz dem Kœnigl. Minister des Unterrichts erstattet von der philosophischen Facultæt der Kœnigl. Friedrich-Wilhelms-Universitæt in den Jahren, 1869 und 1880. Berlin, Ferd. Duemmlers Verlagsbuchhandlung, 1881, 8vo. pages, 83, see pp. 49, 81 sq.

11. Albert Duruy in the Revue des Deux Mondes issue of February 15, 1884, p. 845 sq. See pp. 888, 870 sq.

12. Lukourgos against Leokrates 79. Cap. 19. 158 pag. Steph.

13. January 18, 1854, quoted from the newspapers of the day. The oration is printed in the Southern Literary Messenger, vol. 20, p. 278, see p. 283.

14. Edwards A. Park. Address on life &c., of Leonard Woods, p. 28.

15. R. C. Jebb. The Attic orators from Antiphon to Isaeus. Introduction p. lxxxiii.

16. Tacitus Germania, 8.

17. The ἐφηβεία See Gaston Boissier in the Revue des Deux Mondes, issue of March 15, 1884, pp. 319, 320.

18. Thoukudides II. 40, pag. Steph.

19. Epist. to Corinthians I., 6: 19.

20. A. C. Swinburne, dedication of Atalanta in Calydon, 55, 56.

A HYMN TO LIBERTY.

WRITTEN BY DIONUSIOS SOLOMOS, OF ZANTE, IN THE MONTH OF MAY
1823.

Libertà va *cantando* ch'è'sì cara.
Come sa chi per lei vita rifiuta.

Dante Purgatorio, I. : 71 72.

I know thee by the trenchant gleaming
  Radiant from thy battle sword,
I know thee by that eye whose beaming
  Rules the earth as victor Lord.

Sprung from hero bones that scattered
  Hallow every Grecian vale,
With thy pristine soul unshattered,
  Spirit of Freedom Hail all Hail!

Buried in them thou didst languish
  Lost in shame and woe and fear,
Waiting till to end thine anguish
  "Come to me" should greet thine ear.

But that hour came slowly, slowly;
  Near thee silence reigned alone;
Terror shadowed all things holy;
  Round all slavery's chains were thrown.

Hapless thou! all gladness banished,
  But one cheer thy fancies keep;
To recall thy glories vanished,
  Tell thy tale of eld and weep.

Waiting, hoping that each morrow
  Words of liberty would bear,
While thy hands in bitter sorrow
  Beat the cadence of despair,

And thy low voice "Is my measure
  Not yet filled with suffering," saith,
Answer from yon heavens' azure,
  Moanings, clanging fetters, death.

Then thine eyes were raised, dim, blotted
  With the tears of sorrow's store.
On thy garment folds were clotted
  Trickling blood and Grecian gore.

Stained with crimson, spite of danger,
  All unknown in unknown lands,
Thou didst go to sue the stranger
  For the help of his strong hands.

Alone thou wentest and with mortal
  Anguish camest back alone,
Never easily the portal   ·
  Opens to want's plaintive tone.

Nowhere rest. One loved to hear thee,
  While his heart with pity yearned;
One with promises to cheer thee
  Scorned thee when thy back was turned.

Others laughed to see the waters
  Of thy woe swell round thee high,
" Back and find thy sons and daughters,
  Back to them," the monsters cry.

Over mountain, mead and river
  Thy retreating footstep flies,
Where the funeral shadows quiver
  Of illustrious memories.

Low was bowed thy head and wearing
  Furrows scored by anxious strife,
As the beggar's who despairing
  Groans beneath his load of life.

Hark; Thy sons march out to battle,
  With one spirit praying all,
'Mong the deaths that round them rattle,
  To live victors or to fall.

Sprung from hero bones that scattered
  Hallow every Grecian vale,
With thy pristine soul unshattered,
  Spirit of Freedom Hail all Hail!

Skies that with the fruit and flower
  Greenly draped thy native wild
To adorn a tyrant's dower,
  Looked upon thy zeal and smiled.

Smiled and lo a cry infernal
  Through earth's bosom pealed along;
Answering with a strain supernal
  Rang thy Rhegas' battle song.[1]

Thee with words of welcome greeted
  Every land where patriots dwelt;
And in shouts each tongue repeated
  What each heart so warmly felt.

Thee like stars with music sphery,
  Greets Ionia's starry band.
Pledge of joy heart felt and cheery
  Every islet lifts her hand.

Though each island wears her fetters
  Forged with skill and closely now
And each bears in branded letters
  " False liberty" upon her brow.

With a soul born love outspoken
  Greets the land of Washington,
Glad that she her bonds has broken,
  That her freedom she has won.

While the Western lion tosses
  Haughtily his head and mane,
From his tower a welcome crosses
  The blue sea 'twixt thee and Spain.

Then the pard of Britain's islands
  Pauses, startled, in his path,
Against Russia's dim blue highlands
  Growls the utterance of his wrath;

Shows in every nervous motion
  How his limbs are clad with might,
And o'er Ægæa's mimic ocean
  Glares his eye with meteor light.

From his haunt in clouds untrodden
  That eagle's eye is fixed on thee,
Whose claws are crimsoned, pinions sodden
  In the blood of Italy.

Swooping down with hate and wonder
  In circles each of narrower span,
Croaks and screams the bird of plunder
  To destroy thee if it can.

And thou all the while unshrinking
  Strugglest on forgetting fear,
Silent to those threats nor thinking
  Of the sounds which meet thine ear.

As some rocky cliff where dashes
  Every streamlet soiled with clay
Down to its moveless foot and crashes
  Into flakes of foamy spray,

Which the clouds are thickening under,
  Raining hail upon its breast
While the tempests throb and thunder
  Round its great eternal crest.

Woe, triple woe, to them whose labor
  Thy divine impulse shall brave,
Who withstand thy lifted sabre,
  Who oppose thy falling glave.

From her ravaged den outbursting
  Toward her young, the wild beast ran
'Thwart the hunter's circle, thirsting
  For the red life-blood of man.

On and on her maddened sally
  Through the woods a pathway traced;
Up the mountain, through the valley,
  Spreading terror, death and waste.

Waste and death and terrors lashing,
  Thou didst bid thy progress be;
From its sheath the sabre flashing
  Nobler courage gives to thee.

See the pain before thee whitening,
  Tripolitza's leaguered wall;
Now destruction's bolt of lightning
  Thou art burning to let fall.

Thine eye, with generous exultation,
  Scorns the foeman near and far,
Through the battery's diapason,
  Through the combat's mad hurrah.

Stalking on, around thee prowling,
  As to fright thee with their noise,
Listen to the direful howling
  Of ten thousand men and boys.²

Wailing lips and eyelids clouded
　Soon shall mark the living few
Who lament the dead, unshrouded,
　Of that motley slaughtered crew.

On they come; the heavens brighten
　With the red of battle's glare,
Guns are levelled, muskets lighten,
　Swords flash whirring through the air.

Ho! the struggle so soon ended,
　And our losses how so small;
I see the foe ranks broken, blended,
　Flying to the castle's wall.[3]

Count them, numberless the cravens,
　Crowded on each other's track.
Fated carrion food for ravens,
　With your wounds upon the back.

In your fortressed shelter tarry
　For inevitable doom,
Not enough? then let night carry
　Forth your answer through the gloom.[4]

They answer, and begins another
　Battle din which o'er the plain,
Mount to mount its distant brother
　Wildly echoing rolls again.

I hear the musket's rolling clatter,
　I hear the clash of sword and sheath,
The axe and club, the thud and spatter,
　I hear the grinding gnash of teeth.

Night of horrors, none can number
　Woes which clog the struggling breath,
Night of fear which knew no slumber
　But the nightmare sleep of death.

The scene, the place, the hour, all saddened,
　Shout and cheer and mob like crowd,
War's resolve, soul steeling, maddened
　Battle's surgy, smoky cloud.

Streams of lightning, groans of thunder,
　Bursting through the midnight fogs,
Show the gates of Hell asunder
　Waiting for the Othman dogs,

Opened wide, and thence emerging
  Throngs of naked figures pressed,
Shadowy sire and son and virgin,
  Shadowy infants at the breast.

Black the funeral masses hover
  And the swarming spirits tread,
Black as the pall's enfolding cover
  On the last, the narrow bed.

And they all from every quarter,
  All came rising from the tomb,
Who in Moslem rage of slaughter
  Met the hero martyr's doom.

As the fallen sheaves when reapers
  Cut the harvest fields of grain,
These awakened ghostly sleepers
  Seemed to cover all that plain.

Not a starry beam descended
  As the spirits upward sped,
And they toward the castle wended
  With the stillness of the dead.

So beneath the moon's pale crescent,
  In the forest's leafy night;
When the vale lies phosphorescent
  In a stream of vaporous light;

When the low toned zephyrs rustle
  Through the tendril bordered way,
While above the branches justle,
  Sweeping shadows fitful sway.

Eagerly they scan the places
  Where the blood pools stiffened lie,
And through blood in weird embraces
  Dance with hoarse sepulchral cry.

And each dance impassioned presses
  Closely to the Grecian band;
Each a warrior's breast caresses
  With his death chilled icy hand.

Through the vital members thrilling
  Falls the touch of that caress,
And destroys all grief, instilling
  Rage and hatred merciless.

Then the battle choir engages
  In a yet more awful glee,
As the tempest's fury rages
  O'er unbroken wastes of sea.

Blows are hailing hither, thither,
  And each blow a death sent call;
All are striking reckless, whither,
  But no second stroke need fall.

Every limb is reeking, flowing,
  'Tis as if the soul would fly,
And from hatred's fiery glowing
  Strives its wingèd strength to ply.

But the heart beat pulses coldly
  In the bosom's sluggish calm,
While more fiercely still and boldly
  Falls the sabre swinging arm.

Not a thought the spirit enters,
  Nor of earth, nor sea, nor air,
All in all for each one centres
  In the crowded combat there.

Such the whirl of mad endeavor,
  You might well be sure, I ween,
None from those two bands would ever
  Leave alive that battle scene.

See them hopeless, hero hearted,
  Harvest in death's crimson crop;
How from member member parted,
  Heads, hands, feet before them drop.

Cartridge boxes, steel in shivers,
  Brain clots reeking from the knife,
And the battered trunk that quivers
  With the thrill of parting life.

Not a fleeting thought is given
  To the slaughtered in the fray;
On, still on. Have ye not striven
  Long enough? Cease, cease to slay.

Recreant to his post or willing,
  Though death struck to yield, not one;
Tireless seems the task of killing,
  And the conflict but begun.
  C

But the dogs now few and daunted,
  Allah shout, with Allah die;
Fire! Fire! rises, chaunted
  As the Christians' battle cry.

Fire, and the while they shouted,
  Lion like they fought and bled,
Till the infidels were routed,
  Howling Allah, as they fled.

Everywhere an anguished moaning,
  Curses mixed with fear and prayer,
There was wailing, there was groaning,
  And death's ruckle everywhere.

Once so many! the ball's whistle
  Sings no longer past their ears,
Graveless all in grass and thistle,
  While four times the dawn appears.

And the blood each hillock drenches,
  Stream like rolls each valley through,
And the guiltless herbage quenches
  All its thirst with blood, not dew.

Breeze of morning, dewy, balmy,
  On the crescent breathe no more,
Leave the heathen star[s] and calmly
  On the cross thy blessings pour.

Sprung from hero bones that scattered
  Hallow every Grecian vale,
With thy pristine soul unshattered,
  Spirit of freedom. Hail, all hail!

Corinth's plain, behold it glisten,
  But the sun shines not alone,
Where the vine and the plane tree listen
  To the fountain's purling moan.

And the air no longer treasures
  The low echoes soft and sweet,
Of the flute's responsive measures,
  Of the lambkin's gentle bleat.

As the breaking wave of ocean
  Horsemen surge by thousands on;
But the Pallekar's devotion
  Tarries not its foe to con.

Rise, three hundred, rise returning
  To the spots which once ye knew,
Look upon your children burning
  To behold them so like you.

With their courage flower like faded,
  All the foemen blindly fly,
In the walls of close blockaded
  Acro Corinth, all to die.

Plague and famine, the destroyers,
  The death angel's trusted ones,
Stalk among the languished warriors,
  Arm in arm, two skeletons.

And upon the green sward thicken
  All around, the wretched dead,
Remnants who were left unstricken
  As they battled as they fled.

Freedom, thou divine and deathless,
  Hast all power to work thy will;
On the plain I watch thee breathless,
  Walking stained with blood, and still.

And where yonder shadow lingers,[6]
  There I see in embrace coy,
Maidens with their lily fingers
  Interlaced in choral joy,

Dancing, while love's passion gushes
  From the eye lids parted fold,
And the toying zephyr flushes
  With their ringlet waves of gold.

And my soul with joy is swelling,
  That each virgin breast shall be
To its babe's soft lips a quelling
  Fount of manhood bold and free.

On the grass, among the flowers,
  I dare not lift the reveller's cup,
Songs of freedom in those hours
  I, like Pindar, offer up.

Sprung from hero bones that scattered
  Hallow every Grecian vale,
With thy pristine soul unshattered,
  Spirit of Freedom, Hail all Hail!

Thy foot beneath wax clouds lowering
  Mesolongi's rampart trod,
Christmas morn, when forest flowering,[7]
  Hailed the new born child of God.

Then religion with her torches,
  And her cross led on thy way,
Pointing upward to the porches
  Of eternal, heavenly day.

" Here beside this battle dinted
  Mound," she cried, " Stand, Freedom, fast,"
On thy lips a kiss imprinted,
  And within the Church door passed.[8]

Stands beside the Holy Table,
  While a thickened cloud and dim;
Round and round in hue of sable
  Rises from the censer's brim.

Listens to the chanted psalter,
  Hymns of praise herself had taught,
Sees her saints beside the altar
  With its outpoured radiance fraught.

These who are they pressing nearer
  With the noise of tramping heel?
Thou art listening. Hark, now clearer
  Sounds the ringing din of steel.

And a light, a dazzling whiteness,
  Like the sun's at noon of day,
Robes thee with its beamy brightness,
  Shining with no earthly ray.

Fiery gleams, a flashing cluster,
  Hang from lip, eye, forehead bright,
Hand and foot are clothed in lustre,
  And around thee all is light.

Poised on high thy sabre standeth,
  And thy step thrice forward tends,
As a tower thy form expandeth,
  Another step, the blow descends.

Thou defiant in behavior,
  And thy voice instinct with scorn,
Criest, " Infidels, our Saviour
  And the world's this day was born."

He hath spoken, "Nations tremble,
" I am Alpha, Omega I,[9]
" Can ye before me dissemble?
" Will ye from my anger fly?

" On ye quenchless flame I shower,
" And all fire known to you,
" Of earthly, or of hellish power,
" Is beside it morning's dew.

" A consuming bolt it shooteth
" Hills too high for eye to scan,
" Plain and mountain it uprooteth,
" Felling beast and tree and man.

" All in fiery doom enwreathing,
" Till each thing of life is slain,
" And the wind alone is breathing,
" Through the ashes that remain."

Asketh any? The hand maiden
Of His direful wrath thou art,
Who can meet thee, or who laden
With thy conquered spoils depart?

Thy strong hand earth feels and blesses
A deliverance in her need,
And a vengeful death that presses
On the Christ despising seek.

And the waters feel it pouring
Foam flecked on, and through the air,
Peals the deep voice of their roaring,
Like a wild beast's in his lair.

Fate accursèd fly and welter
In the Acheloös bed,[10]
Struggle valiantly for shelter
From the onslaught fierce and red.

Hasten, for the wave all blinding
Swells as with a tempest sound,
There ye lie, a burial finding
Before ye a death have found.

Curses, howls and groans redouble
From the throat of every foe,
And the gurgling eddies bubble
With the oaths of rage and woe,

And in troops the slipping horses
  Stumble, plunge and frightened rush,
Neighing through the watery courses,
  And the falling bodies crush.

Here an outstretched hand is pleading
  For the succor none can give,
Here one knaws his flesh, unheeding ',
  All save only not to live.

While the heads are surged and drifted,
  With despair all blank, their eyes
Opened staringly, uplifted
  For the last time toward the skies.

All is hushed: its 'whelming torrent,
  Acheloös pours again.
The neighs, the noise of weapons horrent,
  Hushed the groans of dying men."

Oh, to hear deep ocean follow,
  With the roaring of its flood;
See the stifling breaker swallow
  All that sprang from Othman's blood!

Naked corpses, without pity,
  Beaten on the rocks and sands,
Heaped along the seven hilled city,
  Where the Holy Wisdom stands.[11]

Onward by God's curses driven,
  And to see, oh, highest boon,
See those mangled bodies given
  To the " Brother of the moon!"[12]

Let each rock that lieth yonder
  Be a tomb. There let the twain
Freedom and Religion wander
  With slow step, and count the slain.

Now a bloated corpse, unbidden,
  Riseth, stretched upon its face,
While another sinketh hidden
  In the wave, and leaves no trace.

And with wilder rage, the river
  Surges onward in the gloam;
And the swollen waters shiver,
  Tossed in tumult and in foam.

Could I sing such praise ascription
  As triumphant Moses gave
When the God accursed Egyptian
  Fell beneath the wall of wave;

High above the raging breaker
  The thanksgiving psalm be poured,
And before their God and Maker
  All the host with him adored.

Then an echoing strain resounded
  From prophetic Miriam's tongue,
In the timbrel pulses bounded
  Notes by Aaron's sister sung.[13]

All the virgin choirs were dancing
  With wreathed arms and tuneful feet,
Crowned with song and garlands, glancing
  As they too the timbrel beat.

I know thee by the trenchant gleaming
  Radiant from thy battle sword,
I know thee by that eye whose beaming
  Rules the earth as victor Lord.

Yes the earth knows well thy valor,
  Thou wast never conquered there.
Ocean cannot cause thee pallor,
  For its waves thy trophies bear.

With their elemental girtle
  Billows flowing to the land,
Clasp it as a zone of myrtle,
  And thy shining image stand.

In the moaning storm they shudder,
  Hold the palsied ear in check,
And the seaman turns his rudder
  Shoreward from impending wreck.

Then a radiance clear and queenly
  Haloes all the clouds anew,
And the breaking sun serenely
  Gilds the softest sky of blue.

Yes, the land knows well thy valor,
  Never wast thou conquered there,
Ocean cannot cause thee pallor,
  For its waves thy trophies bear.

On its azure fields are bristling
　Like a wood the crowded masts,
With the spiry cordage whistling,
　The sails bellying in the blasts.

Thou thy gathered few, thy truest,
　To the battle line dost call;
Victor still that fleet pursuest,
　Sinking, capturing, burning all.

I see thee, as thine eye, unsated,
　Against two hugh hulks is bent,
From thy hand a lightning freighted
　Bolt of fiery death is sent.[14]

Kindles, streams in flame and deadens,
　And a thunder clap peals high,
And the wave around thee reddens
　As a vat of bloody dye.

Of those crews in order serried,
　No corpse even tells the tale.
Hail, oh martyred and unburied,
　Spirit of the Patriarch, Hail!

Friend and foe in secret union,
　On the morn of Easter met,
Their lips trembling in communion,
　With the mutual kiss were wet.

The bays strewn with love endearing,[15]
　His foot presses now no more,
And his hand ye kissed revering
　Gives no blessing as of yore.

Wail, wail, with the woe that hallows!
　For the church's head is gone,
Mourn ye all, upon the gallows
　Hangs he like a murderer Mourn!

With his white lips shrunk and wasted,
　And mouth gaping, that so late
Christ's own blood and body tasted,
　For those words ye almost wait.

That he spake before the halter's
　Martyr glory crowned his brow,
" Cursèd be the wretch who falters,
　Who can fight and fights not now."

Them I hear, unresting, wondrous
  On the land and on the deep,
" 'Tis they fulmine and the thundrous,
  The eternal lightings leap.

Throbs my heart with fevered spasm,
  But what see I? Lo in peace,
She the godlike, grave phantasm
  Lifts her hands and bids me cease.

Three times her eye westward ranging,
  Europe's utmost border wins,
Then her downward look unchanging,
  Fixed on Greece she thus begins :

Pallekars, a note of gladness
  Rings the war trump to your ears,
'Mong you in the battle's madness
  No knee trembles, no heart fears.

Every foe before you quailing,
  Turns and flies. But even now,
One remains unconquered, paling
  The bay chaplet around each brow.

One—though like mad wolves, the dreary
  Crimson field of strife ye fill
Till with triumph ye grow weary,
  One remains your tyrant still.

Disunion, and her wily offers
  Of a sceptre's regal shine,
That to each she smiling proffers,
  Saying, " Take it; it is thine."

And that sceptre in her keeping
  Seems in sooth a winsome thing,
'Touch it not woe, sorrow, weeping,
  Are the guerdon it will bring.

Never by the tongues of slander
  Let it, Pallekars, be said,
That your hands to hatred pander
  Raised against a brother's head.

Let the thought unspoken perish,
  By the stranger's wish begot,
If a mutual hate they cherish,
  Liberty befits them not.

Leave such brooding; equal splendors
  Of heroic worth embrace,
All the slain who fell defenders
  Of your fathers' faith and race.

By the blood ye gave unsparing,
  For your faith your fatherland,
I adjure ye, all forswearing
  But your love, as brothers stand.

Think of how your faith was plighted,
  Of how much remains to do,
Ever if ye stand united,
  Ever victory follows you.

Heroes in whom fame rejoices
  Now your standard cross uprear,
Summon with accordant voices,
  Look ye kings and princes here,

On this symbol of your pleading,
  Whither all your prayer is sent;
In its cause behold us bleeding,
  With the bitter conflict spent.

Ceaselessly that cross insulting,
  The dogs trample it in pride,
And its sons they kill exulting
  And its holy faith deride.

Shed for it, a red baptism,
  Christian blood and guiltless lies,
That from out night's dark abysm
· Unto you for vengence cries.

Still it cries. It ceases never
  While the ages onward plod,
Hear ye it now? Have heard it ever
  Earthly images of God?

Hear ye not? And all earth pealing
  The blood cry of Abel slain,
'Tis no breath of zephyr stealing
  Through a maiden's tressy train.

Is your will forsooth to set us
  As a stake on policy!
Mind ye that, or will ye let us
  Make ourselves and children free?

If this counsel ye have taken,
  See before you stands the cross,
Strike, ye monarchs, waken, waken,
  Strike and rescue us from loss.

———————

Dionusios Solomos was born in Zante, April 8-19, 1798, and died in Corfu, November 9-21, 1857. His collected poems were published soon after his death. " *Διονυσίου Σολωμοῦ τὰ Ἑυρισκόμενα.*" 1 vol. 8vo., Corfu, 1859, Terzakes.

The events referred to in the foregoing poem are described by George Finlay in his Greek Revolution, vols. 6 and 7 of his history of Greece in Tozer's edition; Thomas Gordon in his Greek Revolutions and Campaigns, and G. G. Gervinus in his Geschichte des 19ten Jahrhunderts, vol. 5. As the last has neither index or table of contents, I add the references. Tripolitza, p. 252. Corinth, p. 371. Mesolongi, p. 364 sq. Kanares' attack on the Turkish fleet at Tenedos, p. 348. The arrest and execution of the patriarch Gregorios, p. 215.

1. Rhegas' song is the

> "*Δεῦτε παῖδες τῶν Ἑλλήνων*
> *Ἄνδρες φίλοι τῶν κινδύνων*
> *Ἡ πατρίς σας προςκαλεῖ*" &c.

2. All over fourteen years of age were in arms.

3. The Castle is a poetical license of Solomos.

4. Current report put the assault at 3 o'clock A. M. It really took place after day break.

5. The star in the crescent on the Turkish flag.

6. Byron's Don Juan Canto III, 86 stanza, 15 verse of ode.

7. Isaiah 35: 1, in the text of the Seventy.

8. Current report kept the churches open. They were in fact closed to confine attention to the walls of the place.

9. Revelations 21: 6.

10. The battle of Christmas and the passage of the river are described by the historians. *i. e.* the Greek Christmas. Our January 6.

11. *Ἡ ἁγία Σοφία* nicknamed the Church of St. Sophia.

12. One of the Sultan's titles.

13. Exodos, Cap. 15.

14. October 29. *i. e.* November 10, 1822, Kanares blew up the Turkish Vice Admiral with sixteen hundred men.

15. The Greek Christians scatter bay branches in their churches at Easter.